My
European
Adventure

THE DR. CAGE CHRONICLES:
MEMOIRS OF A SEX THERAPIST

My
European
Adventure

GRAYSON ACE

4 Horsemen
Publications, Inc.

4 Horsemen Publications, Inc.
1497 Main St. Suite 169
Dunedin, FL 34698
4horsemenpublications.com
info@4horsemenpublications.com

Cover by 4HP
Typeset by MC
Editor Tilda M. Cooke

Library of Congress Control Number:

Print ISBN: 978-1-64450-576-2
Ebook ISBN: 978-1-64450-575-5
Audio ISBN: 978-1-64450-574-8

Chapter 1

A CHANCE ENCOUNTER

I had been daydreaming about this vacation for quite some time, and after my series of recent events, I really needed to just unplug and unwind. I knew I wanted to go to Europe but didn't really know exactly where I wanted to go. I started searching some destinations and then decided that maybe I should just make this trip really exciting and not actually plan out the details.

London seemed like a great place to start, and once I arrived there, I could just decide where my next destination would be. I had two weeks and knew I wanted to end my trip in Prague at that sex house place. I was going for two weeks, so I booked my flight over to London, and my flight home from Prague for two weeks later. I figured each morning when I woke up, I could just decide where to go to next.

I was really tempted to invite Nick to go with me. After finally getting him to fuck me the night before, I think I may have been developing feelings for him. But the point of this trip was to finally experience Europe as a single man—to do what I want with whom I want when I want. He'd be a great companion to take along with me, but that would defeat the whole point of this trip. This trip was about finding myself again—and also seeing how much trouble I could get into.

I booked my flight for the following day, which didn't give me much time to prepare. I was able to reschedule almost all of my sessions and had Rocky handle rescheduling the ones I couldn't get in touch with. Knowing him, he'd still let them show up so he could mess around with them. As long as he billed them properly, I really didn't care.

When I arrived at the airport the following day, my flight was naturally delayed. While waiting for my flight, I went out into the outdoor smoking area to get some fresh air and couldn't believe who I saw.

Nick.

He ran up to me and gave me a big hug, and I was actually kind of happy to see him. He was going to Vegas for the weekend to perform at some club. He said the money was way better in Vegas, and he could make in one night what he made in five days in San Fran. He also said that he couldn't stop thinking about our time together in the VIP room, and honestly, neither could I.

He put out his cigarette and told me to follow him. I grabbed my bag and followed him back into the terminal. He walked toward the men's bathroom, and as we were walking through the entrance, he pushed open the door for the "family restroom" and pulled me inside. The family restroom was basically a private room with a lock on the door, and I knew what he had on his mind.

He shut the door behind me, locked it, pushed my back up against it, and started kissing me. I dropped my bag to the floor and wrapped my arms around him, pulling him closer. He was wearing gym shorts, and I could feel his cock hardening against mine. Someone began knocking on the door, but he didn't even flinch. We kept making out, and I could feel his hands moving down my chest and unzipping my pants.

He pushed my pants down around my knees and dropped to the ground, taking my cock in his mouth. He held onto my hips, pulling my body into his face, and I grabbed onto the back of his head to make his mouth go deeper on my tool. An airport bathroom—one place I had always wanted to mess around but never thought I actually would. This trip was already starting out in a good way, despite the delay.

Nick sucked on my dick for a few minutes before standing up and telling me he wanted to feel my ass again. I really wanted to fuck him this time, but I definitely wasn't going to turn his dick down.

I turned around and faced the door, arching my back and getting my fingers wet to moisten my hole. Neither of us had any lube, so we needed to improvise. Nick pulled his pants down to his ankles and put his hand in front of my mouth to spit on it, rubbing my saliva all over his cock. I knew this was going to hurt like hell, but I didn't even care.

He pressed his head against my hole, slowly forcing it inside. I could tell he was trying to be gentle, but it still hurt anyway. As soon as I felt him all the way inside of me, I let out a really loud moan, and he reached around to cover my mouth. He started thrusting in and out, and it felt just as good as it did the other night. The position was a little awkward, but that actually added to the hotness of the situation.

I started stroking my dick, and I knew I wasn't going to last very long. Nick kept pounding away at my hole, leaning into my neck and kissing me while he was going at it. It definitely felt like more than just fucking with him. There was something else about being with him that I really enjoyed. He started pumping faster, and I could tell he was getting close to cumming.

I reached around and grabbed onto his hips and pushed him out of me. I turned around, got down on my knees, and opened my mouth, sticking my tongue out and stroking my cock. He started jerking off with the head of his cock touching my tongue, and he let out a loud scream as he shot his load straight down my throat. He kept stroking until there was nothing else coming out, and I told him to come down and finish me off.

He got down on the floor in front of me and started slobbing on my knob, and within seconds, I was filling his mouth with my jizz. I couldn't remember if he had ever swallowed me before. Our first few encounters were always me sucking him off and leaving. His mouth was like a vacuum on my shaft, sucking me completely dry.

We got up and put our clothes back on, and he leaned in and gave me a long, romantic kiss. I grabbed my bag and told him that I'd call him when I got back into town. As we snuck out of the restroom while no one was watching, I heard an announcement that my flight was in the final stages of boarding. I gave Nick a quick kiss on his cheek and ran off toward my gate.

Chapter 2

THE LAYOVER

I made it onto my first flight and found my seat. This flight certainly wasn't going to be like the last time I flew home, and the flight attendants definitely didn't look like Scott. It was a smaller plane, and I knew it would be a pretty uneventful flight.

I arrived in in Dallas, and the delay of my first flight caused me to miss my connection to London. The gate agent gave me a voucher for a hotel since the next available flight wasn't for another twelve hours. I was exhausted from the flight and from my little encounter with

Nick, so I was just looking forward to grabbing something to eat and getting some sleep.

I took a shuttle to the hotel, which seemed like a ghost town, and walked inside to check in. The guy working the desk was extremely attractive, and for some reason, he was wearing a tank top, exposing his massive biceps.

"That's quite the uniform for a Marriott," I joked as I approached. The guy behind the counter laughed and said he had just gotten back from working out on his lunch. I almost slipped and said, "You can work me out," but I refrained. I didn't want any of that—I just wanted to get to sleep. He gave me my room key, told me he had a suite available, and did a complementary upgrade.

I got to the room, threw my bag down on the floor, and just lunged onto the bed. I knew I should shower, but Nick didn't cum inside of me, so I was probably fine just waiting until morning. Besides, I'd probably get horny and jerk off thinking about him still a little bit inside of me.

Just as I laid down to go to sleep, I heard a knock on my door. I had no clue who it could have been and was honestly a little annoyed because I was tired. I got up and looked through the peep hole to see if I should even open it—the guy from the front desk.

I grabbed a towel from the bathroom to wrap around me, opened the door, and asked if there was a problem. "No, no problem. Umm, I'm normally not this forthcoming, but you're really hot, and I was wondering if..." I pulled him inside and closed the door, dropping the towel to the floor.

"Go ahead. Suck on it." I wasn't really in the mood but also wasn't going to pass up on a blowjob from a hot guy. I saw down on the edge of the bed, and he tore his shirt off before getting down on his knees in front of me. He grabbed my cock and started stroking it, kissing inside my thighs before making his way to my balls. He stuck his tongue out and started licking my balls, looking up at me while he was stroking my cock.

I laid down on the bed and felt his tongue making its way lower down my balls toward my hole. I hadn't showered, and I assumed it still tasted like Nick's cock. As his tongue reached the top of my hole, he let go of my cock and grabbed my legs, hoisting them over his shoulders. I felt him slip his finger into my hole as he started licking around it before shoving his tongue right inside.

I grabbed onto his hair and pulled his face deeper into my ass as he was tongue fucking my hole pretty hard. He had me going so badly that I knew I was going to end up letting him fuck me. After a few minutes, I leaned forward and pushed his head away from me, dropping down in front of him and pulling his pants down. His cock was only semi-hard and looked to be about ten inches, but I was up for the challenge.

I started sucking on his cock, feeling that monster rip through the back of my throat. I could feel him growing in my mouth, and at one point, I couldn't swallow the entire thing anymore. I sucked on it for about a minute before I wanted him inside of me.

"We need lube." He pulled his pants back on and ran to the little hotel store to grab some. I got back up on the bed and laid down on my back. He came running back in and ripped his pants back off before jumping on top of me. He was still hard when he laid down and started making out with me. I reached down and started stroking his cock, grabbing the lube and rubbing it all over.

He got up and picked my legs up into the air, holding my ankles with one hand and using the other to guide his monster toward my hole. I felt his head pop in, and he slowly entered with the rest, inch by inch until it felt like he was inside my stomach. He let down my legs, holding them with his forearms while he leaned forward to start kissing me while he began thrusting. I was actually kind of surprised that it didn't hurt more, although I was probably still a bit stretched out from Nick.

He pumped his cock in and out of my hole, not letting his mouth drift away from mine. For a second, I wondered who was watching the front desk, but maybe his shift had ended. He fucked me on my back for three or four minutes before grabbing ahold of me and rolling us both over so that he was lying on his back, and I was on top of him. I started bouncing myself up and down on his cock while he grabbed onto mine and stroked it.

I could feel him deep inside of me and kept moaning and holding myself on his chest. I would switch from riding hard and fast to slow and soft, and he would grab onto my hips and raise me in the air to take control. His cock pounding against my hole had me in heaven, and I didn't want it to end.

He pulled my face down toward him and told me he was going to cum. He shoved his tongue down my throat, making out with me, and I could feel his load unleash inside of my hole while he was kissing me and letting out a loud scream at the same time. I raised my body up and kept riding him while jerking my cock, and I shot my load right up on the side of his face. He pushed the cum into his mouth with his fingers and then moved his hand toward my face, feeding me my own cum.

I leaned forward and started making out with him again, eventually feeling his cock fall out of my ass, along with most of his load. I rolled over, and he got out of bed, threw his clothes on really fast, and said his break was over and he needed to get back to work. The door slammed shut behind him, and I realized I never even caught his name.

Chapter 3

RENDEZVOUS

I woke up pretty early the next morning horny as fuck, and I hoped the guy was still at the front desk. I took a quick shower to get the rest of Nick off me and ran out of my room toward the front desk only to be greeted by an older lady who definitely wasn't the guy who fucked me the night before. I was bummed that he was gone, but it wasn't the end of the world because I planned on my next two weeks being an all-out fuck fest.

I packed up my bag and headed back to the airport to check in for my flight. When I checked in, they told me there was an aircraft swap and I had been upgraded to a suite. This was the same thing that happened to me when I went home for a visit, and with this news, I could only hope that there was some hot, sleazy flight attendant who would pay some attention to me mid-flight.

As I boarded the plane, I couldn't believe who the flight attendant was greeting me at the entrance to my suite.

Scott.

I really didn't think that I'd ever see him again after fucking him on my flight the last time I went home to visit my family. I don't think he recognized me at first, probably because I was just one of hundreds of men who he had the same experience with. As I approached the entrance, it must have clicked, and he handed me a glass of champagne. "Welcome back." He had the biggest grin on his face and told me he'd be back to check on me after take-off. As he walked away, he purposely brushed his hand across my dick.

Not even ten minutes had passed after take-off, and I could hear a knock on my suite door. I opened it, and Scott walked in with a bottle of champagne and refilled my glass, closing the door behind me. I stood up from my seat to get close to him, but he placed the bottle of champagne down on the table and walked around me, sitting down in my seat.

"This time, it's my turn."

He grabbed my hand and pulled me over toward him. He pulled me down to his face and started kissing me, his tongue going right down my throat. I quickly got on top of him and straddled him in his seat, grabbed his face, and kept passionately kissing him. He was thrusting his hips as we were kissing. I could feel his hard dick rubbing against me, and I couldn't believe this was really happening—again.

After a few minutes, I slid down onto the floor and pulled his pants off. I left his underwear on and started sucking on his balls and dick through his underwear while rubbing on my own cock. I could tell he was getting really worked up, and he stood up and pulled his underwear all the way off. I put his entire cock in my mouth and started sucking on it, going all the way to the base and back up, teasing the head with my tongue. We hit a little rough patch of air, which forced him back down into his seat, but I never let his dick leave my mouth the entire time. I was stroking his cock, going up and down as my head bobbed up and down. There must have been something about the cabin pressure because I felt like I was giving the best blowjob of my life.

He pushed me back and stood up, grabbed me, and threw me down on the chair so that I was on all fours. He pressed his hard dick up to my ass and reached around to unbuckle my pants, pulling them down around my ankles.

He knelt down behind me, spread my ass cheeks and dug his tongue as deep into my hole as he could go. I started moaning pretty loudly, but thank God for the loud engines drowning out my moans, otherwise someone surely would have barged in to see what was happening. He reached up and covered my mouth, then ate my ass for a few more minutes before saying he wanted to fuck me.

Just like the last time, he pulled a little packet of lube out of his pocket. I could only imagine how many guys he did this to— probably on each flight he worked. He lubed up his cock, and I turned around and sat down on him reverse-cowboy. He let out a moan as his cock entered my hole, and I knew I must have tightened up from the night before. As soon as I felt that he was all the way inside of me, I started bouncing my ass up and down as fast as I could. He held onto my hips as I moved, then pushed my head forward so he could take control, coming out of his seat and slamming his cock into my hole. He pushed me forward and stood up, and I grabbed onto the table in front of my seat. He held onto my hips, and I could feel his cock thrusting in and out of my hole, and I knew he was getting close to blowing.

I told him I wanted him to cum in my mouth, and I pushed him out of my hole, turned around, and got down on my knees so I could start sucking his dick. Almost immediately, he blew his load down my throat, and I started gagging on it a little bit. I kept sucking on his dick until every last drop of his batter was in my mouth, and I started stroking on my own dick. He was so ravenous that I never even grabbed onto my own. Once he was done dripping, he grabbed me by my arms and pushed me against the door. He dropped down in front of me and swallowed my dick, bobbing his head back and forth and stroking my cock as hard as he could.

I grabbed onto the back of his head and shoved by dick straight down his throat, and

I could feel myself unleashing inside of his mouth. He started gagging, and when he pulled his head back and let my dick out of his mouth, I was still cumming and shot more of my load all over his face. He stood up and started kissing me again, then grabbed his shirt to wipe the cum from his face. He grabbed the bottle of champagne, and as he was about to leave through the door, I grabbed his arm and stopped him.

"Last time this happened, you told me that you didn't like topping. What changed?"

He smiled at me and took a quick drink from the bottle of champagne.

"I don't like topping. But I do with you."

He left my suite, and I smiled, my determination to get him inside of me a success.

Chapter 4

LONDON

I touched down in London pretty early in the morning, and even though I was exhausted—both mentally and physically, I didn't want to just go to my hotel and do nothing. London was one of my favorite cities, so full of culture and so many interesting people. I needed to just jump right on board one of the buses and start sight-seeing.

Checking into my hotel, I took a quick shower. At this point, I couldn't even remember how many men had been inside of me over the past 36 hours, so I just needed to freshen up and start anew. I threw on some clean clothes, styled my hair, and ran across the street to the tube to catch the train to the city center.

I loved booking tickets on the double decker buses when I visited Europe. It always seemed like the best way to see a city—hopping off the bus whenever something looked interesting, browsing around the area, and then hopping back on to the next area. It was like having a tour guide but also having the freedom to explore how I see fit.

I always began my trips to London at the Tower Bridge. So many people got confused and think that the beautiful bridge that's always shown in London skyline shots is the actual London Bridge. But in reality, the London Bridge is nothing to look at. The Tower Bridge, however, was this beautiful architectural masterpiece that had so much history behind it.

I grabbed a coffee at one of the gift shops and just browsed around, looking at what the local vendors were selling and, of course, did some people watching. European men were just better looking than Americans, and with this being my first time here as a single man, I really wanted to find out if they were as talented in bed as they were good looking.

I got back on the bus and decided to head over to the Buckingham Palace stop. I figured maybe I'd catch a glimpse of Harry. Or, better yet, maybe he'd catch a glimpse of me. I got to the Palace and walked along the gates, watching the guards do their serious, boring little routine. Two of the guards crossed each other's paths, and as I was taking a picture and looking at them through my zoom lens, I noticed they actually said something to each other as they were walking. I found that interesting because I knew they weren't supposed to speak at all while they were on duty. They walked past each other a second time, and this time I noticed one of them look over, and I swore he looked right at me. I shrugged it off, though. I was probably just having another one of those weird guard fantasies.

I walked the grounds of the palace for about another hour and could feel the coffee starting to run through me. I found a public bathroom, or what seemed to be a public bathroom, opened the door, and went in. I got up to the urinal and unzipped my pants when I heard the door open up behind me. A Palace Guard walked up to the urinal next to me and started to pee. I glanced over out of the corner of my eye and could see his massive uncut cock. I figured every man I ended up fucking around with on this trip would be uncut, and although I'm not a huge fan of uncut dicks, a dick's a dick.

I finished peeing, zipped up my pants, and flushed the urinal. I went to turn to walk away and caught a glimpse of the guard's face, then realized this wasn't a coincidence. It was the guard that I caught talking to the other one. He turned toward me with his cock still hanging out of his pants. He still had his guard hat on, which was a bit weird, but also kind of hot. He looked down at his cock, and then looked back at me, catching me staring at it.

"It's not going to suck itself," he said in his cute British accent.

I dropped down to my knees and grabbed onto his dick, squeezing it hard and pulling the skin back to expose the head. I started teasing the tip with my tongue, swirling around his head before opening my mouth and letting him inside of me. I kept a hold on his cock because I wanted the skin to stay back. I started rubbing on my own dick because I could feel myself getting hard. His tool was slamming into the back of my throat, and he still kept his full uniform on.

I stood up after a few minutes and unzipped my pants, pulling my hard cock out. He didn't say anything. He dropped down and immediately started gagging on it. I could tell by the way he was sucking on it that he probably didn't have much experience. He was doing a good job with the stroking piece, but the sucking was a bit off. I let him go for a couple minutes and then grabbed his head and told him to bend over the sink.

He stood up, walked over to the sink, and bent over it. I dropped down behind him, spreading his cheeks and diving right into his hole with my tongue. He had a hairy hole, but it actually tasted pretty sweet. I didn't have any lube on me, and I knew he didn't, so I needed to get his hole nice and wet. I kept spitting right into it and rubbing it around with my fingers to make sure he was nice and ready.

I stood up and pushed his back to the sink, grabbing my dick with my other hand and aiming it toward his hole. He reached around and spread his cheeks to make it a little easier for me. He still hadn't made any sounds up until this point, and even when I got my cock all the way inside of him, he didn't let out even a single moan.

I started out slowly because I didn't want to hurt him without having any lube, but he wasn't even grunting, so I gradually started pounding his ass faster and faster. I could tell that he was jerking his own cock, and I reached around at one point to help him out. I could tell that he was getting close because he started jerking faster and faster, and I could feel his hole tightening up a bit. I held my grip on his cock, helping him stroke it, and I heard him make the quietest moan and then saw his load shoot all over the sink.

I let go of his cock, grabbed onto his hips, and started pounding even faster. This time, I could hear him moaning, and I'm sure it was starting to hurt a little bit. Within seconds, I felt my dick unload and start shooting all inside of him. I drained my entire cock inside of his hole before letting it slide out.

He turned around and just looked at me, and I wasn't quite sure what was about to happen. He pulled his pants back up, nodded his head, and walked out of the bathroom. I guess they really do have strict rules to follow.

Chapter 5

IRELAND

I spent two more nights in London getting absolutely wasted and trying to find some guys to hook up with, but for some reason I wasn't having any luck. I pulled up a map on my last night there to decide where to head to next, and it wasn't a hard decision at all—Ireland.

I had always wanted to go to Ireland but had never gotten the chance, so here we go. My mom's family was Irish, and I wanted to see if I could find the town that my grandparents came from. I also had this fantasy of making love to a strong Irishman in an ancient castle, but I'd also settle for someone in my hotel, too.

My European Adventure

The next morning, I took a quick flight over to Dublin, rented a car, and just started exploring the country. I had planned on just staying right in Dublin, but I overheard someone on my flight saying that there was a big festival happening in Galway, so I booked a room and decided to start my trip there.

My first two days in the Galway area were pretty uneventful, but I got to see some really amazing places. The castles in Ireland were gorgeous, and it was hard to imagine normal families lived inside of them. The people in Ireland were also so helpful and friendly, and I couldn't get over how trusting they were.

On my last night, I decided to head to one of the pubs on the main street and just get plastered. I was in Ireland—I needed to live up to its name. I asked a few people on the street where the best pub was and followed their recommendation. When I walked into the pub, it was loud, people were cheersing their beers and singing, and there was a band playing in the back. You would have thought it was St. Patty's Day with the way people were acting, and I wasn't mad about it.

I grabbed a beer from the bar and sat down at a table near the corner, just enjoying what was happening around me. At one point, someone got knocked over next to me and spilled their drink on my feet, and I didn't even care. The atmosphere was so cool and was exactly what I was looking for on this trip.

A few beers later, this extremely masculine red-headed guy came over and sat down at the seat across from me. I smiled at him but was also thinking, *I didn't invite you to sit down.* He sat his beer down on the table and reached his hand across to shake mine and introduce himself. His name was Scott, and he was this burly looking guy: red hair, hair arms, a nice beard, and muscles that were practically bursting out of his plaid flannel.

"I know you from somewhere." He was looking at me a little confused but swore up and down that he had seen me somewhere before. "Are you some kind of doctor?" And with that, I knew exactly why he had sat down at my table. I told him that I was a sex therapist, and he got a huge smile on his face and told me that he had read about me in a medical journal at the college where he taught. He was also a therapist as well as a professor, and he told me that he had his class do case studies on some of my patients.

I couldn't help but be flattered but tried not to make it too obvious. This was extremely reassuring for me, as even being unorthodox, my work was being acknowledged all over the world. He proceeded to tell me that his roommate was a huge fan of my work and asked me if I wanted to come back to his house so he could meet me. I was having a great time at the pub but knew I shouldn't miss an opportunity to be a "celebrity," so we both finished our drinks and headed toward his house.

When we arrived at Scott's house, I was greeted at the door by another very similar looking man named Ryan. He was extremely eager to meet me, and as I walked in, I realized that this most likely wasn't going to be just a normal meet and greet. Ryan poured me a beer, and I sat down on the couch and started talking about my practice with each of them sitting on either side of me.

I felt Scott put his hand on my leg as I was talking, and as I turned to look over at him, Ryan grabbed the back of my head and pulled me toward him to start kissing me. His beard rubbed against my face, and it was actually a bit of a turn on. While we were making out, Scott got down on the ground and pushed the coffee table away from the couch, leaving him with plenty of space in front of me. He started unbuttoning my shirt, opened it up, and started kissing my chest. He grabbed onto my nipples and squeezed, bringing his mouth up to suck on them. I felt him start rubbing my cock through my pants, and I was popping a boner within seconds.

Ryan was a very passionate kisser, shoving his tongue down my throat and occasionally moving down to suck on my neck. Scott kept kissing me all over my chest, and Ryan started making his way down, each of them focusing on one nipple. I sat back on the couch to get comfortable and just let them take care of me. Scott was still rubbing on my dick as I felt Ryan start going lower and lower until he was below my belly button, kissing me right above my pant line. Scott started unzipping my pants while still sucking on my nipple, and I felt Ryan grab onto my cock and pull it out through my briefs.

Ryan held tight to my cock while he teased the head with his tongue, and Scott made his way down to join in. Ryan grabbed onto my pants and pulled them completely off of me and dove down to my balls while Scott started devouring my dick. Ryan somehow managed to get both balls in his mouth, and it felt like he was going to suck my cum right out of them. He went up and started licking the side of my cock, and both of them had their lips on each side, going up and down and occasionally taking turns getting the head into their mouth.

I was in pure heaven just sitting there and allowing them to service me, but I really wanted to see what they were working with. I pushed them away from me and got up off of the couch, telling them both to sit down. I knelt down in the middle of them and started rubbing each of their cocks. They started making out with one another, and I quickly unzipped each of their pants, exposing their massive monsters. I was surprised to see that they were but cut and honestly pretty happy about it. I grabbed onto both of their cocks and leaned over to start on Scott's. I felt it were only fair to suck his dick first since he was the one I met at the pub. I bobbed up and down for a few seconds before moving over to Ryan's. As soon as I put Ryan in my mouth, I could feel him flinch, and I knew he was going to be more sensitive.

I went back and forth, completely deep throating both of them, and then told them to stand up in front of me so I could have easier access. I grabbed both of their dicks and shoved them in my mouth at the same time, and as badly as I wanted to taste their cum, I also wanted to feel both of them inside of me.

I stood up from in front of them and told them to take their shirts off. I ripped mine off and pushed Scott back down onto the couch. I got back down on my knees and started sucking his dick again. Ryan went behind me and I felt him spit on my hole. He spread my cheeks and dove right in with his tongue. His tongue must have been as long as his cock because I swear it felt as if he were fucking me. I started moaning while I was sucking on Scott and at the very moment didn't even care if we actually fucked. Scott stood up and said he wanted a taste, and Ryan sat back down on the couch in front of me while Scott went around for his turn. He dove right in just as far, but I felt his finger slip in, too. I was stroking on Ryan's tool while I sucked it and after a few minutes looked behind me and told Scott to fuck me.

He grabbed a bottle of lube from the table and rubbed it all over his dick and my hole. I felt him press his head against me, and I leaned back to get him all the way inside of me. I never let Ryan's cock out of my mouth, and even when Scott started pounding me, my cock-stuffed mouth was deafening my screams. It felt like Scott's dick was shooting all the way up to my throat, and I was loving every minute of it.

Ryan pulled his dick out of my mouth and leaned forward to kiss me, telling me to jump on. I got up and felt Scott's cock release from my hole's death grip, and straddled Ryan, lowering my hold down while he guided his cock to the entrance. I could tell I was pretty loosened up from Scott, and that monster just went right into the forest. I started riding him like a horse, and I could feel Scott's tongue hitting my hole as it was being plowed. At one point Scott pulled Ryan's cock out of my hole to give it a break and suck on it for a minute, putting it back in so I could continue.

Scott stood up behind me and placed his hand on my back, pushing me forward into Ryan so our chests were together. I felt him stick some more lube in my hole, and then felt as he guided his monster's head against my hole with Ryan still inside of me. Ryan wrapped his arms tightly around me and started kissing me, almost as if he knew how much it hurt and was trying to take away the pain.

I felt Scott's head enter my hole, and he slowly pushed the rest of himself inside of me. I was breathing pretty hard, and then I held my breath until I could tell that he couldn't go any farther. These two obviously had done this before because they both knew the right thing to do to make me comfortable. Scott probably sat there for two minutes without moving to allow me ass to adjust, and when I could tell it was the right time, I started moving my body to create some friction.

Ryan was still holding on tightly to me while Scott started taking over and pumping his cock. They took turns taking control, and this was probably one of the greatest feelings in the world. I really wanted them to both finish like this, and I started moving my body again with their movement, and they literally both said they were about to cum at the same time. I felt them each start pumping harder, and when they started blowing their loads it was like a firehose had been shoved up my ass. I could immediately feel their cum dripping out of my hole, and they both kept fucking me until they had gotten every last drop.

Scott pulled out first, followed by Ryan, and the load gushed out of my hole and all over Ryan's cock. Scott stood me up and then got down on the couch next to Ryan. They pulled me in front of them, leaned forward, and started sucking on my balls and dick. I grabbed my dick and started stroking it, both of them sticking their tongues out. Scott reached around and slipped a couple of his fingers in my hole, and I started blowing my load all over their faces and mouths. Ryan leaned in and began sucking my dick again, then turned toward Scott to make out and swap my load. I leaned down and joined in, and we were all making out with each other, getting a little bit of my own cum in my mouth.

I jumped in the shower, where Scott followed, dropping down and giving me another blowjob. He said he couldn't get enough of the taste of my cum and wanted more. Ryan joined in a few minutes later and sucked Scott's cock while Scott sucked on mine, and I have no clue how, but I completely filled Scott's mouth with my load again.

Scott walked me back to the pub, and we had a few more drinks before calling it a night.

He told me to come back and visit anytime, and I was definitely going to take him up on the offer.

Chapter 6

GREECE

I decided to leave Ireland the morning after my rendezvous with Scott. I felt like the two of them were the perfect end to Ireland, and I most certainly looked Scott up on social media so I could keep in touch with him. I had been following a few really hot guys on Instagram for quite some time and saw that they were in Greece, so I decided that would be my next stop.

I started my trip in Athens but quickly hopped a ferry over to Mykonos. The term "Greek God" wasn't even doing the place justice. When I got to the resort, it was nothing but the most gorgeous men with bronze skin and chiseled muscles, just like the statues of Greek mythology. Walking around the pool area was making my little six pack look like nothing.

Laying my towel down on a pool chair, I ordered a cocktail from the waiter. Even the waiters were walking around shirtless and had the most gorgeous bodies I had ever seen. I literally had to pinch myself to make sure I wasn't dreaming. I spent the majority of the day just lying there and man watching, and I was about to leave and head to my room to get ready for dinner when one guy in particular caught my eye.

He had just laid down on a chair across the pool, and from my angle, it was as though he were lying there just inviting me to come get on top of him. He was wearing a gold speedo with his legs spread and what appeared to be a huge package. He was absolutely ripped and had wavy blonde hair that I just wanted to pull on.

I grabbed my items and headed over to the other side of the pool to talk to him. I asked him if anyone was sitting next to him and put my stuff down on the chair. I laid down with my sunglasses on, pretending not to notice that he rolled over and stared me up and down, stopping to focus on my chest. I smiled and looked over at him.

"You like what you see?" I asked. I'm not sure why I was being the pompous one—he was the gorgeous one in this situation. He nodded his head, so I leaned over and told him to follow me. We both grabbed our stuff, and I held onto his hand as we made our way to my room.

We got into the elevator and the door barely even closed before he had me slammed against the mirror, making out with me. The feeling of his chest against mine was like rubbing against a cheese grater—he was that ripped. I couldn't help but move my hands all over his body—he was the hottest guy I think I had ever met.

The elevator door opened, and we ran down the hallway to my room. I was fumbling with my key card and dropped it on the ground because I so nervous. I bent over to grab it, and when I looked up, I noticed he had moved his hips forward so I would be eye level with his package.

It. Was. Something.

If he didn't already have a boner, then he had something quite impressive in there, and I was about to find out. I managed to get the door unlocked and went into the room, heading straight over to the bed. He pushed me down and got on top of me, kissing me and thrusting his cock against mine. Now I could tell that he was getting hard, and I was damn near popping out of my shorts.

I rolled him over and got on top of him, so I could take control. We were still making out, but I started letting my hands drift down toward his Speedo. I grabbed onto his tool and couldn't believe what I was holding in my hand. I started kissing my way down his chest until I got to his suit and started kissing around his cock. I pulled his Speedo down, exposing his monster standing at full attention. I didn't even wait. I shot my mouth straight up and onto his dick and let that thing annihilate the back of my throat. I was gagging and drooling and wanted to feel him pushing at the back on my neck. He grabbed onto my hair and helped pull my head up and down on that thing.

I pulled off my own bathing suit while I was choking on him and crawled up to facefuck him. I pushed a pillow under his head to give him some support, and he grabbed onto my ass cheeks so he could pull me toward his face faster and faster. I could feel my dick going down his throat and I felt like I was getting a blowjob from a celebrity. I was still having a hard time believing this Adonis was on my bed.

I flipped myself around so we could 69, and I licked two of my fingers and shoved them into his hole. He was sucking on my balls and making his way to my ass, letting his tongue barely caress the edge of it before going back to my cock where I was plowing his mouth. I lifted his legs under my arms so my tongue could drive straight into his hole, and it got so wild that we ended up rolling on our side and falling off the bed. We both started laughing and then jumped right back into action.

I laid down on my back and told him to get on top of me. He straddled my cock, leaning forward and kissing me while rubbing his hole on my member. I reached over and grabbed the lube so I could get inside of him, but before I could even open the lid, he had me entering. I had his ass so moist from eating it that we didn't even need any lube. My cock inserted so easily it was like a hot knife through butter. That thing was gliding in and out of him so smoothly, and why wouldn't it? He was perfect.

I grabbed ahold of his dick and stroked it while he was riding me, leaning forward so I could suck on it while I was inside of him. He reached back and stuck a few fingers in my hole, and I could feel myself growing even more inside of him. The way he was moving his hips was unlike anything I had ever felt, and I swear in that moment I was in love.

Just kidding.

This was just one of the best fucks of my life. I rolled him over without letting my dick out of his hole and held his legs in the air so I could really power fuck him. He was stroking his monster as I plowed his hole, and the noises coming out of him were like euphoria. He said he wanted to get back on top, so I grabbed onto him and rolled back over so he could ride me again.

I hoisted his hips up so I could get deep, and when I knew he was getting ready to cum I let him back down and leaned forward so I could start sucking his cock again. He was moving his hips so fast that I could tell I was getting close. The second he let out a scream and I felt his load filling my mouth, I unleased inside of his hole. I swallowed his load while he kept riding me, and he leaned forward to start making out again.

I had to place this in one of the top five fucks of my life. I asked him to spend the night with me, which he immediately agreed to. I held him in my arms the entire night, and at one point I woke up to him sucking on my cock, blowing my load all over his face. I fell asleep but planned on getting him inside of me in the morning before he left.

But when I woke up, he was gone, and I honestly didn't know if it was all just a dream.

Chapter 7

PRAGUE

I wasn't sure how anything about this trip could top what had happened in Greece. I never even got his name, and part of me wanted to stay longer to find him and learn more about him. I knew it was reality, but I still really felt like the entire night was a dream.

Ready for the final leg of my journey to Prague, I couldn't have been more excited about finding out if the sex house I had seen in pornos was real. Just the thought of it made me a bit nervous, but this was going to be a once in a lifetime opportunity, and I was really hoping it was a real place, especially since it was the only reason I was wrapping up my trip in Prague.

I couldn't find any last-minute flights to Prague but wasn't going to miss this opportunity, so I ended up chartering a private jet. It cost me more than my practice makes in a month, but I knew it was going to be worth it. I was secretly hoping for a sexy male flight attendant—fucking in a private jet would have been way better than my time with Scott, the flight attendant, but unfortunately it was an elderly lady. She was very friendly, but I obviously wouldn't be getting any action on this flight.

I arrived in Prague, checked into my hotel, and immediately began researching the sex house online, but I couldn't find any information about it. I couldn't understand why it was so hard to locate this place. If it were as real as it was, and with Prague being an orgy mecca, it had to be easy to locate.

Deciding to do some bar hopping to hopefully get some information on finding this brothel, I went into three different bars, which I assumed to be gay bars, but no one seemed to know what I was talking about. There was one more bar on the edge of town, and it seemed a little sketchy, but I decided to give things one last try. As I approached the bar, I almost left because of how rough it looked. It almost appeared to be inside an old barn, and there were only a few cars in the parking lot, but I had to give it a chance.

I walked through the front door and was greeted by a "cashier" behind a partition. I thought it was a little odd to have to pay a fee to get into a bar, but I really didn't have a choice. It cost me the equivalent of 20 bucks to get in, which was outrageous, but I handed him the money and started to walk around the corner as he told me to "have fun" in his language.

When I walked around the corner, I couldn't believe my eyes. I was there! I had found the sex house, and it was absolutely real! There were only a few other customers, but I knew I was going to get my money's worth.

I stood there for a few minutes just taking it all in. There was a "map" on the wall which looked like it tried to explain what happened in each of the two rooms. There were two guys over against the side wall getting their dicks sucked at a dual glory hole. Aside from that, the rest of the room was open and like my own private oasis.

On one side of the room were three more glory holes, two to get blowjobs and one for a hand job. On the other side wall were two openings with guy's bottom halves hanging out of with their legs and feet held above. One was up high to finger and eat his hole, and the other was down lower to fuck. On the back wall of the first room were two guys who were bent over just waiting to get nailed from behind. There was one more glory hole next to them. I wasn't quite sure what it was for but assumed it might be for fucking.

I started rubbing my dick and headed over to the guy who was higher on the wall with his legs in the air. His hole looked so inviting and I wanted to taste it. I unzipped my pants and let my dick out so it could grow and started kissing his cheeks. I spread his ass open and tapped on his hole a little bit, watching him react before diving in with my tongue. I could hear him moaning on the other side of the wall. I had one finger inside the entire time I was eating him and eventually slipped another one in. I let go of his cheeks so I could stoke my cock a little bit but didn't get too carried away because I knew there was more to enjoy.

I made my way over to the glory hole wall where the other two guys were still getting blown. I stuck my dick through the third opening and felt someone start stroking on it. I leaned down and asked if he could suck on it, which he immediately started. I grabbed onto

the guy's arm next to me to hold himself up—
the blowjob was that good. He leaned over to
me so we could start making out, but a worker
quickly ran up to us to separate us. Apparently,
we didn't read the rules, and we weren't allowed
to play with each other. I let the guy suck on my
dick for a few more minutes, stroking it and
occasionally working his way down to my balls
before moving on.

I moved my way over to the other wall
where the two guys were bent over, practically
waiting for me. I knelt down behind lefty and
started eating his ass while I rubbed righty's
hole with my finger. I grabbed some lube off
the stand—there was lube available at every
opening—moistened my cock and shoved it
right into lefty. I kept a hand on righty's ass
the entire time, fingering him when I could
concentrate enough to do so. Lefty's hold was
super loose, but it still felt pretty amazing. I
imagined that the two were bent forward
and making out with one another—because

what else would they do? Although they were probably so used to it by now that they just laid there waiting for their shift to end.

I switched over to righty after a few minutes. His hole was way tighter, and he got really squirmish as I entered him. I got my head in and could tell he was struggling, so I gave him a few seconds to adjust before going the rest of the way in. I reached over and slipped two fingers into lefty and started pounding away. It was hard to try and keep doing this to both of them, so I eventually took my hand back and just focused on my plowing. I grabbed onto his legs and went to town, listening to him scream on the other side of the wall.

I was so ready to blow my load but knew there was another room, and I wanted to see what that was about. I pulled my cock out and walked over to the next door, where I was greeted by another cashier. He told me that I needed to wait because the room was already occupied, so I took a seat and slowly stroked my dick while I watched the other two guys make their way around the room. The cashier approached me while I was waiting to collect my money. This time, it was closer to 60 bucks. I didn't know what I was walking in to, but based on what 20 bucks got me, it had to be good.

After I waited about ten minutes, the door opened, and as I walked down the hall and into the main part of the room, I couldn't believe what I was seeing. This was the craziest contraption I had ever seen. There was a table in the middle of the room with a giant box on it. There was a guy inside the box, and he could either be on his back or on his stomach with his legs down. On top of the box was another guy—ass hanging off the edge. Behind the table was another box standing upright with a gloryhole, but this box was meant to be behind you and could be moved so that it was touching you or not.

There was an old man waiting at the table for me. He asked me exactly how I wanted all of the men set up and told me to get into position when I was ready. I entered the room ready and was rock hard and told him I wanted the guy on the table on his back with his legs propped in the air, and that I wanted the glory hole box behind me moved forward so I could get fucked.

I got up to the table and waited for the box behind me to be moved closer. I turned around to look and saw about eight inches of cock hardness sticking out of the hole, and the old man adjusted it so it was level with my ass. He moved the box forward and then grabbed onto the hard cock to guide it into my hole. His dick felt amazing, and I started moving forward and backward, letting him slide in and out.

I moved forward a bit, and the old man came back and grabbed my own cock to shove it into the hole of the guy on the table. I started thrusting in and out, shoving my cock in as the back cock came out, and vice versa. It was always such an amazing feeling to fuck and get fucked at the same time. I leaned forward to start eating the guy's ass on top of the box but honestly couldn't focus enough to get inside of him. The other feelings were taking over my body, and I just wanted to focus on what was going on with my bottom half.

I was able to last for a good five or six minutes before getting close. I started pumping the guy's hole faster and harder, and as I did, I could feel the box behind me get closer with the eight inches going deeper into my hole. I let out a loud burst as I busted my load deep inside the guy's hole, and the sensitivity was almost too much to handle. I wanted the full experience, though, so I didn't stop moving until I could feel the guy behind me unleashing inside of me.

I heard him start moaning and could feel him flooding my hole with his warm cum. I kept moving until we were both completely drained, and then the old man came back over to move the box from behind me. He pointed up at the guy on top of the box jerking off, and I climbed up the box and started sucking his cock. I felt bad that I had ignored him, but I'm sure he didn't mind. I didn't even have his dick in my mouth for ten seconds when he started shooting his load, and I swallowed every last drop.

I threw on my clothes and headed back to my hotel. On the cab ride back, I got online and booked my flight back to San Francisco for the following day.

My mission in Europe was over and was definitely a huge success.

Author Bio

Grayson Ace has had his fair share of sexcapades, and figured why not write about them? Recently divorced, he is re-discovering himself (and plenty of hot men) and creating many new sexy adventures along the way. If you like what you see, please leave a review, and you never know....you may end up in one of the stories!

GraysonAce.com
Facebook: Grayson Ace
Instagram: graysonaceofficial
Twitter: @GraysonAce1

4 Horsemen Publications

LGBT Erotica

Leo Sparx
Before Alexander
Claiming Alexander
Taming Alexander
Saving Alexander

Erotica

Ali Whippe
Office Hours
Tutoring Center
Athletics
Extra Credit
Bound for Release
Fetish Circuit

Dalia Lance
My Home on Whore Island
Slumming It on Slut Street
Training of the Tramp
The Imperfect Perfection
72% Match
It Was Meant To Be... Or Whatever

4HORSEMENPUBLICATIONS.COM